GRADE 1

The Little Mermaid
小美人魚

Original Author   Hans Christian Andersen
Adaptors   Louise Benette / David Hwang
Illustrator   Ekaterina Andreeva

WORDS
350

Let's Enjoy Masterpieces!

All the beautiful fairy tales and masterpieces that you have encountered during your childhood remain as warm memories in your adulthood. This time, let's indulge in the world of masterpieces through English. You can enjoy the depth and beauty of original works, which you can't enjoy through Chinese translations.

The stories are easy for you to understand because of your familiarity with them. When you enjoy reading, your ability to understand English will also rapidly improve.

This series of *Let's Enjoy Masterpieces* is a special reading comprehension booster program, devised to improve reading comprehension for beginners whose command of English is not satisfactory, or who are elementary, middle, and high school students. With this program, you can enjoy reading masterpieces in English with fun and efficiency.

This carefully planned program is composed of 5 levels, from the beginner level of 350 words to the intermediate and advanced levels of 1,000 words. With this program's level-by-level system, you are able to read famous texts in English and to savor the true pleasure of the world's language.

The program is well conceived, composed of reader-friendly explanations of English expressions and grammar, quizzes to help the student learn vocabulary and understand the meaning of the texts, and fabulous illustrations that adorn every page. In addition, with our "Guide to Listening," not only is reading comprehension enhanced but also listening comprehension skills are highlighted.

In the audio recording of the book, texts are vividly read by professional American voice actors. The texts are rewritten, according to the levels of the readers by an expert editorial staff of native speakers, on the basis of standard American English with the ministry of education recommended vocabulary. Therefore, it will be of great help even for all the students that want to learn English.

Please indulge yourself in the fun of reading and listening to English through *Let's Enjoy Masterpieces*.

漢斯・克里斯汀・安徒生

Hans Christian
Andersen
(1805–1875)

Hans Christian Andersen was born in Odense, a small fishing village, on the island of Funen, Denmark, on April 2, 1805. His father was a poor cobbler. Even so, he was a literary man of progressive idea, who enjoyed reading and encouraged Andersen to cultivate his artistic interests.

Andersen started writing when he was a university student. After his first novel Improvisatore, which was based on his trip to Italy in 1833, received critical acclaim, Andersen earned even greater fame as a writer with his first book of fairy tales, *Tales Told for Children*. Later, Anderson became a well-loved writer of children's literature. By the time of his death in 1875, he had published a total of around 130 tales.

Andersen wrote many books that have been considered as the best works of literature for children, such as *The Little Mermaid, The Ugly Duckling, and The Emperor's New Clothes*. Despite many difficulties, Andersen rose above them to tell us enchanting stories. In his works, Anderson zealously intertwined his lyrical writing style with manifestations of beautiful imaginary lands and humanism.

After living a solitary life, Andersen died alone. On his funeral day, all the Danish people wore mourning clothes, and the king and queen attended his funeral. Andersen was also an active poet. His beautiful poems and fairy tales are still loved by people around the world.

The Little Mermaid was based on Andersen's unconsummated love for a woman he had loved all his life.

On her 15th birthday, the little mermaid is allowed, for the first time, to go to the surface of the water. There, she catches sight of a prince, who is celebrating his birthday on a ship, and falls in love with him. As she watches the prince, a sudden storm sweeps over the sea and destroys the ship. However, the little mermaid saves the unconscious prince from the shipwreck.

To be near the prince, the little mermaid strikes a deal with a witch. In exchange for her voice, she is turned into a human and goes to the prince's palace. However, the prince marries the princess from the neighboring country, not realizing that the mute mermaid is the one who rescued him from the storm. In despair, the little mermaid throws herself into the sea and becomes a nymph of the air.

Andersen wrote many great fairy tales, and *The Little Mermaid* remains the most widely read of all his works, touching the hearts of children and adults, all around the world.

HOW TO USE THIS BOOK
本書使用說明

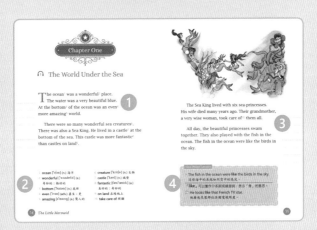

1 Original English texts

It is easy to understand the meaning of the text, because the text is rewritten according to the levels of the readers.

2 Explanation of the vocabulary

The words and expressions that include vocabulary above the elementary level are clearly defined.

3 Response notes

Spaces are included in the book so you can take notes about what you don't understand or what you want to remember.

4 One point lesson

In-depth analyses of major grammar points and expressions help you to understand sentences with difficult grammar.

🎧 Audio Recording

In the audio recording, native speakers narrate the texts in standard American English. By combining the written words and the audio recording, you can listen to English with great ease.

Audio books have been popular in Britain and America for many decades. They allow the listener to experience the proper word pronunciation and sentence intonation that add important meaning and drama to spoken English. Students will benefit from listening to the recording twenty or more times.

After you are familiar with the text and recording, listen once more with your eyes closed to check your listening comprehension. Finally, after you can listen with your eyes closed and understand every word and every sentence, you are then ready to mimic the native speaker.

Then you should make a recording by reading the text yourself. Then play both recordings to compare your oral skills with those of a native speaker.

HOW TO IMPROVE READING ABILITY

如何增進英文閱讀能力

1 *Catch key words*

Read the key words in the sentences and practice catching the gist of the meaning of the sentence. You might question how working with a few important words could enhance your reading ability. However, it's quite effective. If you continue to use this method, you will find out that the key words and your knowledge of people and situations enables you to understand the sentence.

2 *Divide long sentences*

Read in chunks of meaning, dividing sentences into meaningful chunks of information. In the book, chunks are arranged in sentences according to meaning. If you consider the sentences backwards or grammatically, your reading speed will be slow and you will find it difficult to listen to English.

You are ready to move to a more sophisticated level of comprehension when you find that narrowly focusing on chunks is irritating. Instead of considering the chunks, you will make it a habit to read the sentence from the beginning to the end to figure out the meaning of the whole.

❸ Make inferences and assumptions

Making inferences and assumptions is part of your ability. If you don't know, try to guess the meaning of the words. Although you don't know all the words in context, don't go straight to the dictionary. Developing an ability to make inferences in the context is important.

The first way to figure out the meaning of a word is from its context. If you cannot make head or tail out of the meaning of a word, look at what comes before or after it. Ask yourself what can happen in such a situation. Make your best guess as to the word's meaning. Then check the explanations of the word in the book or look up the word in a dictionary.

❹ Read a lot and reread the same book many times

There is no shortcut to mastering English. Only if you do a lot of reading will you make your way to the summit. Read fun and easy books with an average of less than one new word per page. Try to immerse yourself in English as often as you can.

Spend time "swimming" in English. Language learning research has shown that immersing yourself in English will help you improve your English, even though you may not be aware of what you're learning.

CONTENTS

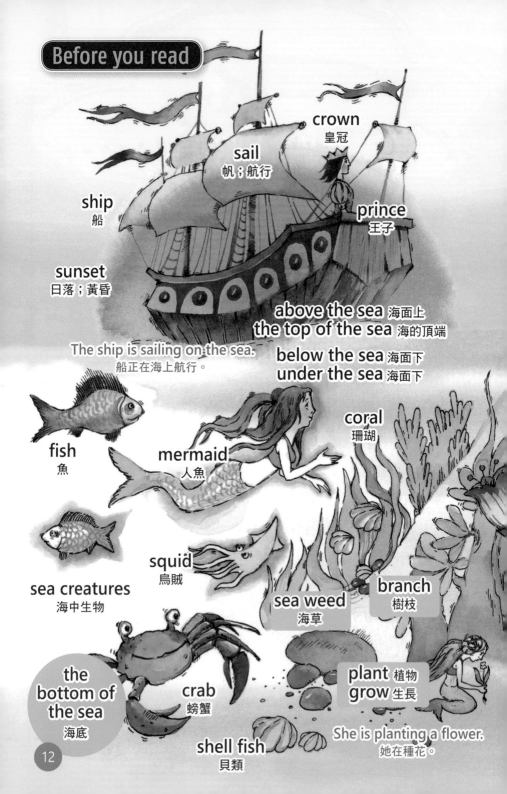

Before you read

crown 皇冠

sail 帆；航行

ship 船

prince 王子

sunset 日落；黃昏

above the sea 海面上
the top of the sea 海的頂端

The ship is sailing on the sea.
船正在海上航行。

below the sea 海面下
under the sea 海面下

fish 魚

mermaid 人魚

coral 珊瑚

sea creatures 海中生物

squid 烏賊

branch 樹枝

sea weed 海草

the bottom of the sea 海底

crab 螃蟹

plant 植物
grow 生長

She is planting a flower.
她在種花。

shell fish 貝類

12

The ocean is an amazing world.
海洋是一個奇妙的世界。

rock
岩石

beach
海灘

Children are playing
on the beach.
孩子們在海灘上遊玩。

sand
沙灘

rest
靠；臥

A mermaid is
resting on a rock.
人魚靠在岩石上。

starfish
海星

sea shell
海貝

sea castle
海中城堡

deep
ocean
深海

palace
皇宮

sea plant
海底植物

sea princess
海公主

statue
雕像

sea
garden
海中花園

sea king
海中國王

13

Chapter One

🎧 [1] The World Under the Sea

The ocean[1] was a wonderful[2] place.
The water was a very beautiful blue.
At the bottom[3] of the ocean was an even[4]
more amazing[5] world.

There were so many wonderful sea creatures[6].
There was also a Sea King. He lived in a castle[7] at the
bottom of the sea. This castle was more fantastic[8]
than castles on land[9].

---

1 **ocean** [ˋoʃən] (n.) 海洋
2 **wonderful** [ˋwʌndəfəl] (a.)
　奇妙的；極好的
3 **bottom** [ˋbɑtəm] (n.) 底部
4 **even** [ˋivən] (adv.) 甚至；更
5 **amazing** [əˋmezɪŋ] (a.) 驚人的

6 **creature** [ˋkritʃə] (n.) 生物
7 **castle** [ˋkæsl] (n.) 城堡
8 **fantastic** [fænˋtæstɪk] (a.)
　美好的；奇妙的
9 **on land** 在陸地上
10 **take care of** 照顧

The Sea King lived with six sea-princesses. His wife died many years ago. Their grandmother, a very wise woman, took care of[10] them all.

All day, the beautiful princesses swam together. They also played with the fish in the ocean. The fish in the ocean were like the birds in the sky.

Each sea-princess was very special. But the youngest[1] was the prettiest[2]. Her skin was so white and clear, and her long hair flew[3] smoothly[4] in the sea. She seemed like[5] other girls on land. But she had a tail[6] like a fish.

Every day the little mermaid[7] liked to stay[8] in her garden, and grew[9] red flowers. She never went out of[10] the sea.

1 **youngest** 年紀最輕的
2 **prettiest** 最漂亮的
  (pretty-prettier-prettiest)
3 **flow** [flo] (v.) 流
  (flow-flew-flown)
4 **smoothly** [ˋsmuðlɪ] (adv.) 平滑地；
  流暢地

5 **seem like** 看似
6 **tail** [tel] (n.) 尾部
7 **mermaid** [ˋmɝˏmed] (n.) 美人魚
8 **stay** [ste] (v.) 停留；逗留
9 **grow** [gro] (v.) 種植
  (grow-grew-grown)
10 **out of** 自……離開

One day, a statue[11] fell[12] to the bottom of the
ocean. It looked like[13] a beautiful boy.
She asked her grandmother, "What is it?"
"It is a statue from a ship. It is like the people
above[14] us," said her grandmother.

The little mermaid loved the statue.
She planted[15] some beautiful trees near it.
The branches[16] floated[17] around the statue's face.
He was always smiling in the deep[18],
deep ocean.

11 **statue** [ˈstætʃʊ] (n.) 雕像
12 **fall** [fɔl] (v.) 落下
(fall-fell-fallen)
13 **look like** 看起來像
14 **above** [əˈbʌv] (prep.)
在⋯⋯上面
15 **plant** [plænt] (v.) 種植

16 **branch** [bræntʃ] (n.) 樹枝
17 **float** [flot] (v.) 浮
18 **deep** [dip] (a.) 深的

🎧 3

    The little mermaid loved stories about[1] the land. She always said to her grandmother, "Tell me a story about the land above us." Her grandmother told about beautiful ships, towns, and the people above.

1 **about** [ə'baʊt] (prep.)
  關於；對於
2 **perfume** ['pɝfjum] (n.)
  香味；芳香

3 **want to** 想要
4 **only** ['onlɪ] (adv.) 僅僅；只
5 **such** [sʌtʃ] (a.) 如此的
6 **be going to** 將要

"Really? The flowers have perfume[2]?
The fish in the trees can sing?" she asked.
She didn't know about birds.

"I want to[3] see the people, the fish,
and the flowers," she said.
"You can go when you are fifteen," her
grandmother said.
"Fifteen!" thought the mermaid. "I am
only[4] nine now. It is such[5] a long time to
wait."

The little mermaid swam to her oldest
sister. "Sister!" she said. "You're going to[6] be
fifteen next year. Tell me all about the land
above."

One Point Lesson

It is such a long time to wait!
要等那麼久的時間！

such a 在口語中可以用來修飾名詞，指「如此；實在」。

e.g. It is such a good day. 這真是美好的一天。

At last[1], it was her oldest sister's birthday.

"It was wonderful," she said.

"I saw so many things. I lay[2] on a beach in the moonlight[3]. I saw a town and some people. It was so exciting.[4]" The little mermaid listened carefully[5].

One year passed by[6] quickly[7]. Now, it was the second sister's turn[8]. She swam up[9] a river. She saw palaces[10], and green hills[11]. She saw people laughing[12], and children playing.

---

1 **at last** 最後；終於

2 **lie** [laɪ] (v.) 躺；臥 (lie-lay-lain)

3 **moonlight** [ˋmun͵laɪt] (n.) 月光

4 **exciting** [ɪkˋsaɪtɪŋ] (a.) 令人興奮的

5 **carefully** [ˋkɛrfəlɪ] (adv.) 仔細地

6 **pass by**（時間）過去

7 **quickly** [ˋkwɪklɪ] (adv.) 快地

8 **turn** [tɝn] (n.)（依次輪到的）機會

9 **swim up** 往上游 (swim-swam-swum)

10 **palace** [ˋpælɪs] (n.) 皇宮

11 **hill** [hɪl] (n.) 小山；丘陵

12 **laugh** [læf] (v.) 笑

13 **feel envious** 覺得羨慕

"It was interesting," she said. "I want to go again tomorrow." Again, the little mermaid felt envious[13].

21

Every year, each sister had to[1] tell the other sisters about the world above. They loved to[2] see new things, but quickly became[3] bored[4].

But the little mermaid wanted to see everything. She said to her sisters, "Tell me another[5] story."

"We told you everything. We have no more[6] stories. It isn't interesting anymore[7]," they said.

---

1 **have to** 必須 (= must)

2 **love to** 熱愛

3 **become** [bɪˋkʌm] (v.) 變得

4 **bored** [bɔrd] (a.)
  無聊的；厭倦的

5 **another** [əˋnʌðɚ] (a.) 另外的

6 **no more** 不再有

7 **anymore** [ˋɛnɪmɔr] (adv.)
  再也（不）

8 **look up** 往上看

9 **care about** 在乎；介意

10 **forever** [fəˋɛvɚ] (adv.) 永遠

11 **say to oneself** 對自己說

Every night, she looked up[8], and thought, "When will my turn come?"

"I want to be fifteen. My sisters don't care about[9] the world above the ocean. I will love it forever[10]," she said to herself[11].

Comprehension Quiz Chapter One

A Write down the English of each word.

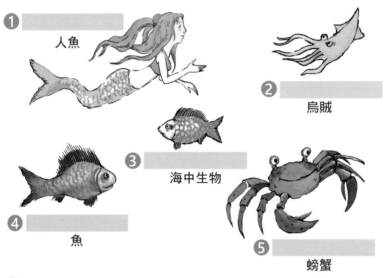

❶ _____
人魚

❷ _____
烏賊

❸ _____
海中生物

❹ _____
魚

❺ _____
螃蟹

B True or False.

T **F** ❶ At age 15, the little mermaid saw the top of the ocean.

T **F** ❷ The little mermaid had four sisters.

T **F** ❸ The little mermaid likes to grow orange flowers.

T **F** ❹ The little mermaid planted trees around the statue of the boy.

C Write down the past tense of each verb.

❶ The ocean *is* → _____ a wonderful place.

❷ Their grandmother *takes* → _____ care of them.

❸ She *swims* → _____ so well in the sea.

❹ A beautiful statue *falls* → _____ to the bottom of the ocean.

D Fill in the blanks with the given words.

> like other girls   the prettiest
> feet   to play   like a fish

The little mermaid was ❶_____.

But she wasn't ❷_____. She didn't have any

❸_____. She had a tail ❹_____. She liked

❺_____ in her garden.

mast
帆柱

People are having a birthday party.
人們正在辦一場生日宴會。

sail
帆

The birthday boy is
a handsome prince.
過生日的男孩是一位英俊的王子。

handsome
英俊的

She has a beautiful voice.
她有很美的嗓音。

voice
聲音

princess
公主

deck
甲板

decorate
裝飾

laugh
笑

laughter
笑聲

They are laughing together.
他們一起笑著。

The ship is decorated with shells.
這艘船用貝殼裝飾。

wave
波浪

Waves are rough.
波浪洶湧。

storm
暴風雨

The wind is strong.
風很強勁。

turn over
翻覆

sink 沉沒

The ship is turning over.
船正在翻覆。

building
建築物

The prince is sinking.
王子正在往下沉。

broken
毀壞的

The mast is broken.
帆柱損壞了。

bell 鐘

save/rescue
拯救

The bell is ringing.
鐘在響。

The little mermaid is
rescuing him.
小美人魚正在救他。

temple
神殿

hide oneself
自己躲藏起來

People are
standing over him.
人們站在他的上方。

behind
在……後面

lie 躺

The little mermaid is hiding
herself behind the rock.
小美人魚把自己藏身在岩石後面。

He is lying on a beach.
他躺在沙灘上。

27

· Chapter Two ·

🎧 6 # The World Above the Sea

The little mermaid finally[1] became fifteen. "I am fifteen! I am fifteen!" she shouted[2] excitedly[3]. Her grandmother put some white flowers in[4] her hair.

Then, she swam to the top of the sea. The sun was setting[5] now. It was full of[6] red and orange clouds. "How beautiful!" she thought.
    She could see a ship sailing[7] on the sea. She swam close to the ship. She heard music and laughing.

---

1 **finally** [ˈfaɪnl̩ɪ] (adv.) 最後
2 **shout** [ʃaʊt] (v.) 呼喊；喊叫
3 **excitedly** [ɪkˈsaɪtɪdlɪ] (adv.)
   興奮地；激動地

4 **put . . . in** 把……放進
5 **set** [sɛt] (v.) 下沉；落下
   (set-set-set)
6 **be full of** 充滿

There was also a young man. He was a prince[8].
Everyone was having a birthday party[9] for him.
They all looked very happy.

The little mermaid watched the prince for
hours[10].

7 **sail** [sel] (v.) 航行
8 **prince** [prɪns] (n.) 王子
9 **have a party** 舉辦宴會
10 **for hours** 好幾個小時

Suddenly, a storm[1] came. The sky was very angry, and the wind was very strong. The waves[2] were becoming very rough[3].

But the little mermaid was not scared[4].
It was great fun[5] for her to swim in the storm,
but not for the ship. Suddenly, the wind broke[6]
the ship's mast[7]. A few seconds later[8], the ship
turned over[9] into the sea.

The little mermaid could see many people
swimming in the rough sea.
"People cannot swim very well. Where is the
prince? I must help him," thought she.

After some searching[10], she found[11] the
prince. He was sinking[12] deep into the ocean.
She took him to the top of the sea, and looked
into[13] his handsome face all night long[14].

1 **storm** [stɔrm] (n.) 暴風雨
2 **wave** [wev] (n.) 海浪;波浪
3 **rough** [rʌf] (a.) 劇烈的
4 **scared** [skɛrd] (a.) 恐懼的
5 **fun** [fʌn] (n.) 樂趣
6 **break** [brek] (v.) 折斷;破裂
7 **mast** [mæst] (n.) 帆柱;桅杆
8 **a few seconds later** 不久

9   **turn over** 翻覆;傾覆
10 **search** [sɜtʃ] (v.) 尋覓;找
11 **find** [faɪnd] (v.) 找到
    (find-found-found)
12 **sink** [sɪŋk] (v.) 下沈
    (sink-sank-sunk)
13 **look into** 細細檢視
14 **all night long** 一整夜

By[1] morning, the storm was finished[2]. In the sunlight[3], the prince looked more handsome. His eyes were still[4] closed.

"Please don't die[5]. You must live," she said.

Close to the beach, there was a small building. She took the prince very close to the building. She laid[6] him on the beach.

Suddenly, some bells[7] began to ring[8]. Some young girls came out of[9] the building.

One of the young girls saw the prince on the beach. She came to him. Then she ran[10] to get help[11].

After a few[12] minutes, many people took the young prince away[13]. The mermaid suddenly[14] felt very sad.

1 **by** [baɪ] (prep.) 在⋯⋯之前
2 **finished** [ˈfɪnɪʃt] (a.) 結束了的
3 **sunlight** [ˈsʌnˌlaɪt] (n.) 日光
4 **still** [stɪl] (adv.) 還；仍舊
5 **die** [daɪ] (v.) 死
6 **lay** [le] (v.) 放 (lay-laid-laid)
7 **bell** [bɛl] (n.) 鐘；鈴

8 **ring** [rɪŋ] (v.) （鐘）鳴；響 (ring-rang-rung)
9 **out of** 來自
10 **run** [rʌn] (v.) 跑；奔
11 **get help** 尋求幫助
12 **a few** 一些
13 **take away** 帶走
14 **suddenly** [ˈsʌdn̩lɪ] (adv.) 忽然

One Point Lesson

• Then she ran **to get** help. 於是她去找人幫忙。

「**to + 動詞原形**」形成不定詞，可以用來表示行為的目的。

• She stayed home **to watch** TV.
她留在家裡是為了要看電視。

33

🎧 9

After the little mermaid returned home, her sisters cried[1], "What did you see? What did you see?"

But the little mermaid said nothing[2]. She was too sad to speak.

One day, she finally[3] told her sisters. One of the sisters took her to his palace[4]. She found her prince again.

Now she thought, "I can come here at any time.[5]"

She spent many evenings there.

1 **cry** [kraɪ] (v.) 叫喊
2 **nothing** [ˈnʌθɪŋ] (pron.) 無;無事
3 **finally** [ˈfaɪnlɪ] (adv.) 最後;終於
4 **palace** [ˈpælɪs] (n.) 皇宮
5 **at any time** 在任何時候
6 **after some time** 過了一段時間
7 **decide to** 決定
8 **forever** [fəˈɛvɚ] (adv.) 永遠地;永恆地
9 **soul** [sol] (n.) 靈魂
10 **foam** [fom] (n.) 泡沫

After some time[6],
she had so many questions
about people. She decided to[7]
ask her grandmother.

"Grandmother, can people
live forever[8]?" she asked.

"No, they can't. They don't
live very long. But people have
souls[9]. Their souls live forever.
We can live for three hundred
years. Then, we become the
foam[10] in the ocean."

One Point Lesson

She was **too** sad **to** speak. 她難過得說不出話。

「**too ... to**」的意思是「太……，以致於不能……」。

The pepper was **too** hot **to** eat.
這辣椒太辣，根本吃不下去。

"I want to have a soul.
I want to live like a person,"
said the little mermaid.
"Can I never have a soul?
How[1] can I get[2] a soul?"
she asked her grandmother.

Grandmother said,
"There is only[3] one way[4].
A man must fall in love
with[5] you. Then, you must
marry[6] him."

1 **how** [haʊ] (adv.) 如何
2 **get** [gɛt] (v.) 得到；獲得
  (get-got-got)
3 **only** [ˈonlɪ] (a.) 僅；只
4 **way** [we] (n.) 方法
5 **fall in love with** 愛上
6 **marry** [ˈmærɪ] (v.) 結婚

7 **impossible** [ɪmˈpɑsəbl̩] (a.)
  不可能的
8 **dream of** 夢想；渴望
9 **hate** [het] (v.) 厭惡；討厭
10 **better** [ˈbɛtɚ] (a.)
  改善的；好轉的

"But this is impossible[7]. You have a beautiful tail. But people think it is ugly. No man will want to marry a mermaid. Do not dream of[8] the world above the sea anymore. You will only be sad."

She looked at her tail and thought, "I hate[9] it. I want to have two legs. I want to marry the prince."

"Just be happy," Grandmother finally said. "Live happily for three hundred years. This evening, there will be a big party. You will feel better[10] then."

One Point Lesson

There is **only** one way. 只有一個辦法。
You will **only** be sad. 到頭來你只會傷心難過。

---

only 作「唯一的；僅有的」時，是形容詞；作「僅；只會」時，是副詞。

e.g. She is my **only** friend. 她是我唯一的朋友。
e.g. This is for teenagers **only**. 這只開放給青少年。

The party in the deep sea castle was fantastic.
Many different kinds[1] of shells[2] decorated[3] the walls.

1 **kind** [kaɪnd] (n.) 種類
2 **shell** [ʃɛl] (n.) 貝殼
3 **decorate** [ˋdɛkəˌret] (v.) 裝飾
4 **merman** [ˋmɝˌmæn] (n.)
  雄人魚（單數）
5 **ballroom** [ˋbɔlˌrum] (n.) 舞廳
6 **best** [bɛst] (a.) 最好的
7 **think of** 想到；記起
  (think-thought-thought)

8 **sadly** [ˋsædlɪ] (adv.)
  傷心地；悲哀地
9 **leave** [liv] (v.) 離開
  (leave-left-left)
10 **own** [on] (a.) 自己的
11 **in peace** 平靜地
12 **anything** [ˋɛnɪˌθɪŋ] (pron.)
  無論任何事物
13 **witch** [wɪtʃ] (n.) 女巫

The mermaids and the mermen[4] danced together in the ballroom[5]. And they sang together. They all had beautiful voices. But the little mermaid sang the best[6]. Everyone loved her singing. For a short time, the little mermaid felt happy.

Then, she thought of[7] the prince. She became sad again. Sadly[8], she left[9] the party. She went to her own[10] place —her garden. There, she could cry in peace[11]. She thought, "I love him. I will do anything[12] for him. And I want to have a soul. I will go to the sea witch[13]. She can help me."

One Point Lesson

◌ She could cry **in peace**. 她可以靜靜地哭泣。

---

in peace 兩個字放在一起當副詞用，意義同 **peacefully**（平靜地）。某些名詞前加上介系詞，便有副詞的修飾功能。

on purpose 故意地 (= purposely)
in a hurry 趕快 (= hurriedly)

A Finish the Crosswords.

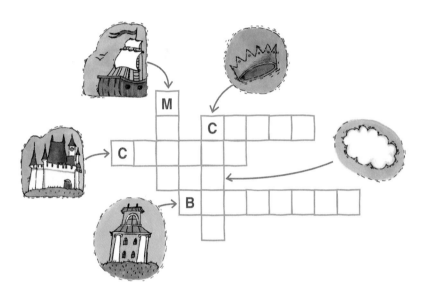

B Fill in the blanks with the given words.

> beautifully   soul   decorated

❶ For the party, sea shells _____ the beautiful walls.

❷ At the party, the little mermaid sang _____.

❸ The little mermaid wanted have a _____.

C Choose the correct answer.

❶ What was happening on board the ship?
(a) There was a fire.
(b) There was a wedding.
(c) There was a birthday party.

❷ Why did the mermaid want to become a person?
(a) She hated swimming in the ocean.
(b) She wanted to have a soul.
(c) She wanted to have a human baby.

D Rearrange the sentences in chronological order.

❶ On board the ship, people were having a party.

❷ The mermaid lay the prince on the beach.

❸ The ship turned over into the sea.

❹ One of the sisters took the little mermaid to the prince's palace.

_____ → _____ → _____ → _____

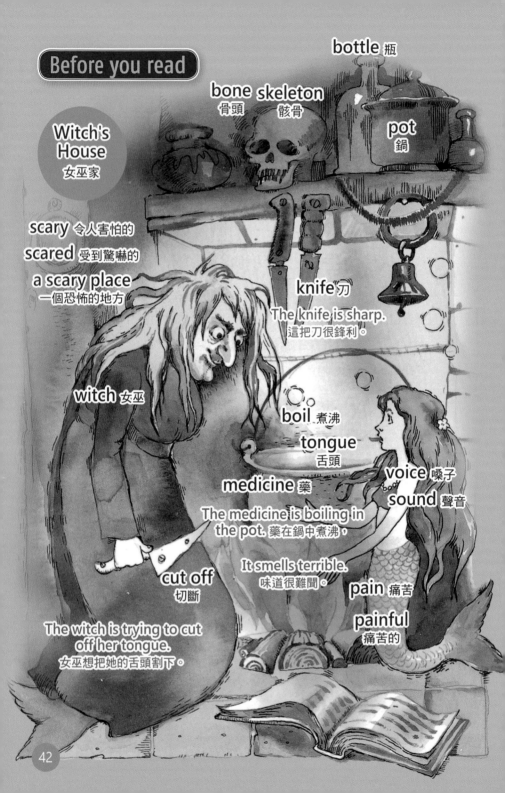

bottle 瓶

bone 骨頭 skeleton 骸骨

pot 鍋

Witch's House 女巫家

scary 令人害怕的
scared 受到驚嚇的
a scary place 一個恐怖的地方

knife 刀
The knife is sharp.
這把刀很鋒利。

witch 女巫

boil 煮沸

tongue 舌頭

medicine 藥

voice 嗓子
sound 聲音

The medicine is boiling in the pot. 藥在鍋中煮沸，

It smells terrible. 味道很難聞。

pain 痛苦

cut off 切斷

painful 痛苦的

The witch is trying to cut off her tongue.
女巫想把她的舌頭割下。

42

clap 拍手
She clapped her hands.
她拍手。

wave 揮手
She waved at them.
她對他們揮手。

turn 轉向
She turned, and saw him.
她轉身，看到他。

shout 喊叫
She shouted at her sisters.
她對姊妹們大聲呼喊。

run 跑
She is running.
她在跑。

smell 聞；嗅
She smelled a flower.
她嗅了一朵花。

bleed 流血
Her finger bled.
她的手指流血了。

stare 凝視
He is staring at something.
他盯著某樣東西猛瞧。

express 表達
Her hands expressed much.
她的雙手很能表情達意！

miss 想念
She missed him very much.
她非常想念他。

fall in love 愛上
The prince fell in love with a princess.
王子愛上了一位公主。

save 拯救
He saved his friend's life.
他救了朋友一命。

Chapter Three

The Witch

The little mermaid went to look for[1] the witch. She swam to a very dark place. She thought, "This is a very scary[2] place. But I must go." She continued to swim. She saw many whirlpools[3]. She had to be careful[4]. A whirlpool could suck her into[5] its middle[6].

After some time, she saw the witch's house. It was made from[7] many dead[8] sailors'[9] bones[10]. The sea princess felt very afraid[11]. She almost[12] left.

Then, she thought, "The prince! And my soul! I must not be afraid." She swam toward[13] the house. She even saw a young mermaid lying dead. This shocked[14] the little mermaid very much.

Again, the little mermaid wanted to leave. But the witch came out of the door, and said, "Don't go! I know why you came."

1 **look for** 尋找

2 **scary** [ˈskɛrɪ] (a.) 駭人的

3 **whirlpool** [ˈwɝl͵pul] (n.) 漩渦

4 **careful** [ˈkɛrfəl] (a.) 小心的

5 **suck into** 吞沒；捲入

6 **middle** [ˈmɪdl̩] (n.) 中央

7 **be made from** 由……建造

8 **dead** [dɛd] (a.) 死亡的

9 **sailor** [ˈselɚ] (n.) 水手

10 **bone** [bon] (n.) 骨頭

11 **afraid** [əˈfred] (a.) 害怕的

12 **almost** [ˈɔl͵most] (adv.) 幾乎

13 **toward** [təˈwɔrd] (prep.) 朝；向

14 **shock** [ʃɑk] (v.) 使震驚

🎧 13

The little mermaid followed[1] the witch into
the bone house.

"You are a stupid[2] girl. Your family will be
very sad. But I will give you your wish[3]," said the
witch.

"I will give you something to drink⁴. You must take it with you. Tomorrow morning, before sunrise⁵, you must swim to land. Sit down on a beach. Then, drink the medicine⁶. Your tail will disappear⁷. You will grow two legs. But it will be very painful⁸. It will be like knives⁹ in your legs and feet. But you will move beautifully. You will dance so well. Can you bear¹⁰ the pain¹¹?"

1 **follow** [ˈfɑlo] (v.) 跟隨
2 **stupid** [ˈstjupɪd] (a.) 愚蠢的
3 **wish** [wɪʃ] (n.) 願望
4 **drink** [drɪŋk] (v.) 喝
   (drink-drank-drunk)
5 **sunrise** [ˈsʌnˌraɪz] (n.) 日出
6 **medicine** [ˈmɛdəsn̩] (n.) 藥物

7 **disappear** [ˌdɪsəˈpɪr] (v.) 消失
8 **painful** [ˈpenfəl] (a.) 痛苦的
9 **knives** [naɪvz] (n.) 刀
   （knife 的複數）
10 **bear** [bɛr] (v.) 忍受
11 **pain** [pen] (n.) 痛苦

One Point Lesson

◊ I will give you **something to drink**. 我會給你要喝的東西。

「**名詞 + to**」的不定詞：不定詞用來修飾名詞，描述該名詞的作用。

e.g. I have a lot of **things to do**. 我有很多事情要做。

14

The mermaid said to
the witch, "I can do it!"
The witch looked at[1]
her carefully[2].

"Are you sure[3]?" she
asked. "You can never[4]
become[5] a mermaid again.
You can never swim with
your sisters. You can never
see your father or grandmother
again. The prince must marry you. Then, you
can have a soul. But you will die when he
marries another[6] girl. Are you sure?"

1 **look at** 看
2 **carefully** [ˈkɛrfəlɪ] (adv.)
   仔細地；謹慎地
3 **sure** [ʃʊr] (a.) 確定的
4 **never . . . again** 再也不……

5 **become** [bɪˈkʌm] (v.) 變成
6 **another** [əˈnʌðɚ] (a.) 別的
7 **pay** [pe] (v.) 報酬；支付
8 **won't** [wont] will not 的縮寫
9 **need** [nid] (v.) 需要

The little mermaid said, "Yes, I will do it."
But she was so scared.

"Then, you must pay[7] me," said the witch.
"I want your voice. You won't[8] need[9] it. The
prince will love your beauty[10]."

"My voice! Then, how can I speak?"
the mermaid asked.

"That is my price[11]," snapped[12] the witch.
"You are beautiful. Your eyes speak for[13]
you."

"I will do it," said the mermaid.

10 **beauty** ['bjutɪ] (n.) 美
11 **price** [praɪs] (n.) 價格;代價
12 **snap** [snæp] (v.) 怒罵   13 **speak for** 為……發聲
   (snap-snapped-snapped)   (speak-spoke-spoken)

15

The witch started to make the medicine.
She used many awful[1] things in the medicine.
She put in[2] a fish stomach[3]. Then, she put in
crab[4] eyes. Next, she put in squid[5] brains[6].

The medicine boiled[7]. It smelled[8] terrible[9].

"This is the medicine," she said.
"You must give me your tongue[10]."

The princess stuck out[11] her tongue. The witch cut it off[12]. It was very painful. She tried to speak, but could not make any words.

The witch spoke to her again. "Tomorrow morning, before sunrise, do as[13] I said. Then you'll get beautiful feet."

The princess wanted to say, "I will do that." But she couldn't speak. So, she only nodded[14] her head. And she left the witch's house.

1 **awful** ['ɔful] (a.) 嚇人的
2 **put in** 放進
3 **stomach** ['stʌmək] (n.) 胃
4 **crab** [kræb] (n.) 螃蟹
5 **squid** [skwɪd] (n.) 烏賊
6 **brain** [bren] (n.) 腦
7 **boil** [bɔɪl] (v.) 煮沸；沸騰
8 **smell** [smɛl] (v.) 聞
9 **terrible** ['tɛrəbl̩] (a.) 令人討厭的

10 **tongue** [tʌŋ] (n.) 舌頭
11 **stick out** 伸出
    (stick-stuck-stuck)
12 **cut off** 砍斷
13 **as** [æz] (conj.) 按照
14 **nod** [nɑd] (v.) 點頭
    (nod-nodded-nodded)

16

She quickly went back[1] home. Everyone was sleeping. She wanted to go and speak to her sisters. But she could not say one word.

Now, she felt great sorrow[2]. She wanted to cry. Instead[3], she went to the flower gardens. She took[4] flowers from her sisters' gardens. She wanted a memory of her sisters and her home. Then, she left.

The sea princess swam through[5] the water. The morning was coming. She could see everything clearly[6].

---

1 **go back** 回去 (go-went-gone)
2 **sorrow** [ˋsɑro] (n.) 哀痛；悲傷
3 **instead** [ɪnˋstɛd] (adv.) 代替；取代
4 **take** [tek] (v.) 拿；取 (take-took-taken)
5 **through** [θru] (prep.) 穿過；通過

6 **clearly** [ˋklɪrlɪ] (adv.) 清楚地；明確地
7 **reach** [ritʃ] (v.) 到達；抵達
8 **lie down** 躺下；臥下 (lie-lay-lain)
9 **fall down** 跌倒；跌墜 (fall-fell-fallen)
10 **sand** [sænd] (n.) 沙地；沙灘

She swam close to the prince's palace. She reached[7] the beach, and lay down[8] there. Then, she drank the medicine. Suddenly, she felt very sick. It was like a knife in her body. She fell down[9] in the sand[10].

A Write down the English of each word.

1 [_____] 舌頭

2 [_____] 嗓子

3 [_____] 聲音

4 [_____] 痛苦

5 [_____] 痛苦的

B True or False.

T F 1 The witch's house was made from dead sailor's bones.

T F 2 The witch wanted the little mermaid's tail for pay.

T F 3 The little mermaid felt happy when she drank the medicine.

C Fill in the blanks with "so many" and "so much."

There are so *many* wonderful things in the sea.
There is so *much* noise on the boat.

1 The witch put _____ strange things into the pot.

2 The little mermaid has _____ love for the prince.

3 _____ people loved the little mermaid.

4 There is _____ water in the ocean.

D Fill in the blanks with the given words.

scary	suck	witch

The little mermaid went to look for the **1** _____. She
swam to a very dark place. She thought, "This is a very
2 _____ place. But I must go." She continued to swim.
She saw many whirlpools. A whirlpool could **3** _____
her into its middle.

Chapter Four

Her New World

🎧 17

In the morning, the little mermaid woke up[1], and looked at her body. Her tail was gone[2]. Now, she had two legs and two feet.

Then she saw a shadow[3]. She looked up[4]. The prince was standing[5] over[6] her, and staring at[7] her face.

Chapter Four **Her New World**

The prince asked her, "Who are you? Where are you from?"

But she could not speak. So, she just looked deeply[8] into his eyes. At that moment[9], the prince had very strong feelings[10] for her.

The prince said, "You must come inside[11]. You must be[12] very cold."

She stood up[13]. She felt very strong pains in her legs and feet. But she ignored[14] the pain.

The prince took her inside the palace, and also gave her a beautiful dress. She was the most[15] beautiful girl.

1 **wake up** 甦醒
  (wake-woke-woken)
2 **be gone** 不見了
3 **shadow** [`ʃædo] (n.) 影子
4 **look up** 往上看
5 **stand** [stænd] (v.) 站立;站著
  (stand-stood-stood)
6 **over** [`ovɚ] (prep.) 在上面
7 **stare at** 注視;凝視

8 **deeply** [`dɪplɪ] (adv.) 深深地
9 **moment** [`momənt] (n.) 片刻
10 **feeling** [`filɪŋ] (n.) 同情
11 **inside** [`ɪnˋsaɪd] (adv.) 在裡面
12 **must be** 一定是
13 **stand up** 站起來
14 **ignore** [ɪgˋnor] (v.) 忽視
15 **the most** 最;極

A few days later[1], there was a singing contest[2]. So many beautiful women came to sing. They all sang so well[3]. This time was very difficult for the princess.

She thought, "I want to sing for the prince. My voice is more[4] beautiful."

But later, there was dancing. Now, the mermaid could dance for the prince. She danced so beautifully. Her hands expressed[5] so much. Her eyes expressed even more.

Everyone clapped[6] and shouted[7], "Beautiful! Beautiful!"

The Prince couldn't stop[8] watching her.

---

1 **later** [ˈletɚ] (adv.) 稍後
2 **contest** [ˈkɑntɛst] (n.) 比賽
3 **well** [wɛl] (adv.) 很好地
4 **more** [mor] (adv.) 更加地
  （many 和 much 的比較級）

5 **express** [ɪkˈsprɛs] (v.) 表達
6 **clap** [klæp] (v.) 拍手
7 **shout** [ʃaut] (v.) 叫喊
8 **stop + V-ing** 停止（做某件事）
  (stop-stopped-stopped)

After the party, she was always with[1] the prince. She rode[2] with him on a horse. They rode through[3] fresh[4] forests[5] together. They walked beside the calm[6] ocean.

They were always together. But it was always painful for her. Her feet often[7] bled[8]. She always tried to ignore the pain.

1 **be with** 與……一起
2 **ride** [raɪd] (v.) 騎馬
   (ride-rode-ridden)
3 **through** [θru] (prep.) 穿過
4 **fresh** [frɛʃ] (a.) 清新的
5 **forest** [ˋfɔrɪst] (n.) 森林
6 **calm** [kɑm] (a.) 平靜的
7 **often** [ˋɔfən] (adv.) 時常

8 **bleed** [blid] (v.) 流血
   (bleed-bled-bled)
9 **at night** 夜晚
10 **put** [pʊt] (v.) 放；置
11 **those** [ðoz] (pron.) 那些
12 **think of** 想到
13 **hope** [hop] (v.) 希望
14 **be well** 健康；安好

The Little Mermaid

Sometimes, at night[9], she went to the ocean. She put[10] her feet in the sea. It always felt so good.

At those[11] times, she thought of[12] her family. She thought, "I hope[13] they are happy. I hope they are well[14]. I hope they understand me."

One Point Lesson

I **hope (that)** they understand me. 我希望他們能了解我。

在口語用法中，在某些表示「說」或「想」等認知的動詞之後，連接詞 that 常被省略。

e.g. I **think (that)** the boy likes you. 我想這男孩喜歡你。

e.g. He **says (that)** he didn't know about it.
他說他並不知道這件事。

🎧 20

 One night, the little mermaid went to the sea.
She put her feet into¹ the cool² water.
 Suddenly, she saw her sisters.

"Sisters!" she called out[3]. But she couldn't make any sound[4]. So, she waved[5] at them to get[6] their attention[7].

Finally they turned[8] and saw her.

"You are not dead," the sisters said. "We looked and looked for[9] you. We cried so much for you. We are so happy to see you."

"I am so happy to see you too," the little mermaid wanted to say.

Every night, they went to see each other[10].

1 **put A into B** 把 A 放進 B
2 **cool** [kul] (a.) 涼快的
3 **call out** 大叫
4 **sound** [saʊnd] (n.) 聲音
5 **wave** [wev] (n.) 揮手
6 **get one's attention**
   引起某人的注意

7 **attention** [əˈtɛnʃən] (n.)
   注意力
8 **turn** [tɜn] (v.) 轉身
9 **look for** 尋找
10 **each other** 彼此

One Point Lesson

We **are** so **happy to** see you. 我們好高興能見到妳。

be happy + to 不定詞：很高興……

I'm **glad to** meet you again. 再見到你我很高興。
I'm **sorry to** hear that. 聽到那件事我非常遺憾。

The mermaid fell in love with[1] the prince. The prince also loved the mermaid. But it was different.

He loved her like a sister. He did not think of her like a wife. This bothered[2] her very much.

The prince told her a story. "Once[3], I was on a ship. There was a storm. The ship turned over[4] into the sea. The waves threw[5] me onto[6] a beach. A young girl found me on the beach. She saved[7] my life."

"I love only her. But you look like[8] her. Maybe, she sent you to me," he said.

The little mermaid felt very sad. "I saved you. But you don't know," she thought.

---

1 **fall in love with** 愛上
  (fall-fell-fallen)
2 **bother** [ˋbɑðɚ] (v.) 煩擾
3 **once** [wʌns] (adv.) 曾經
4 **turn over** 翻覆

5 **throw** [θro] (v.) 拋；擲
  (throw-threw-thrown)
6 **onto** [ˋɑntu] (prep.) 到……上
7 **save** [sev] (v.) 救
8 **look like** 看起來像

◊ **Once**, I was on a ship. 我曾經待在一艘船上。

once: 曾經；一旦；一次

🅴🅶 **Once** there was a beautiful princess.
從前，有一位美麗的公主。

🅴🅶 I meet my friends **once** a week.
我每星期和朋友們見一次面。

A Fill in the blanks with the given words.

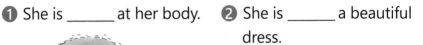

wearing   looking   riding   dancing

❶ She is _____ at her body.

❷ She is _____ a beautiful dress.

❸ She is _____ so beautifully.

❹ They are _____ together.

B True or False.

T F ❶ The mermaid sang beautifully for the prince.

T F ❷ The mermaid was the most graceful dancer.

T F ❸ It was always painful when she walked.

C Rewrite the sentences in past continuous tense.

The mermaid *swam* to the beach.
The mermaid *was swimming* to the beach.

1 The prince stood over her.

→ _____

2 He stared at her face.

→ _____

3 She wore very beautiful clothes.

→ _____

D Rearrange the sentences in chronological order.

1 The little mermaid met her sisters in the ocean.

2 The little mermaid rode on a horse with the prince.

3 The prince found the little mermaid on the beach.

4 The little mermaid put on some beautiful clothes.

5 The little mermaid danced for the prince.

_____ → _____ → _____ → _____ → _____

Before you read

Wedding Ceremony 結婚典禮

wedding 婚禮
marriage 婚姻
marry 結婚

guest 賓客

celebrate 慶祝

best man 伴郎

bouquet 花束

a perfect couple 完美的一對

bride 新娘

cross 十字架

wedding dress 新娘禮服

bridegroom 新郎

candle 蠟燭

flower girl/boy 花童

aisle 走道

walking down the aisle 走上紅毯

A bridesmaid is holding a fan.
有一位伴娘拿著一把扇子。

fan 扇子

bridesmaid 伴娘

68

Wedding Reception 婚宴

festival 喜慶

be filled with 充滿
The party is filled with music and food.
宴會上充滿音樂和食物。

cheerful 歡樂的
joyful 愉快的
The party is joyful.
宴會上一派歡樂。

elegant 優雅的
elegantly 優雅地
They are dancing elegantly.
他們優雅地跳著舞。

band 樂隊
The band is playing music.
樂隊在演奏音樂。

drop 掉下；落下
He dropped a glass.
他摔下了一個玻璃杯。

69

Chapter Five

🎧 ₂₂ Some Terrible¹ News

A short time later, she heard some news. The prince planned to² marry a king's daughter.

"I must go to meet the king's daughter," he said to the mermaid. She felt very sad about this.

"My parents want me to go. I do not want to marry her," he said. This made³ her very happy.

1 **terrible** ['tɛrəbl̩] (a.) 駭人的
2 **plan to** 計畫做……
3 **make** [mek] (v.) 使得
4 **deck** [dɛk] (n.) 甲板
5 **look out** 往外看

6 **appear** [ə'pɪr] (v.) 出現
7 **disappointed** [ˌdɪsə'pɔɪntɪd] (a.) 失望的
8 **yet** [jɛt] (adv.) 然而;但是

"Will you come with me? I want you to sail on the ship with me," he asked.

At night, she sat on the deck[4] of the ship. She looked out[5] into the ocean. Suddenly, her sisters appeared[6]. They swam close to the ship. But they saw a boy on the deck. The sisters swam deep under the water. The little mermaid was so disappointed[7]. Yet[8], she was happy. She could see her prince every day.

One Point Lesson

　My parents **want me to** go. 我的父母希望我去。

「**want + A + to 不定式**」：希望 A……

My mother **wants me to** study all day.
我母親希望我整天念書。

The boat reached[1] a beautiful town. The king's daughter lived in this town[2]. Many people came to the ship, and welcomed[3] the prince. There was a festival[4] all day[5] in the town. All day, the king's daughter did not appear.

But that night she came. The prince saw her face. He knew her face.

"You!" he cried out[6]. "It was you! You saved my life[7]."

1 **reach** [ritʃ] (v.) 抵達
2 **town** [taʊn] (n.) 市鎮；都市
3 **welcome** [ˈwɛlkəm] (v.) 歡迎
4 **festival** [ˈfɛstəvl̩] (n.) 慶祝活動
5 **all day** 整天
6 **cry out** 大叫
7 **life** [laɪf] (n.) 性命
8 **perfect** [ˈpɝfɪkt] (a.) 完美的

9 **beside** [bɪˈsaɪd] (prep.) 在旁邊
10 **complete** [kəmˈplit] (a.) 圓滿的；完整的
10 **smile** [smaɪl] (v.) 微笑
12 **break** [brek] (v.) 破碎 (break-broke-broken)
13 **wedding** [ˈwɛdɪŋ] (n.) 婚禮
14 **mean** [min] (v.) 意味著

The prince looked at the little mermaid.
He said, "Oh! I am so happy now. Everything is
perfect[8]. I love this woman so much. And you are
beside[9] me. My life is complete[10]."

The mermaid smiled[11] at him. But her heart
broke[12] in two. His wedding[13] meant[14] one thing.
She must die.

🎧 24

For the prince and the king's daughter's
wedding, the little mermaid wore[1] a golden[2] dress.
She walked behind[3] the bride[4] in the church.
There was joyful[5] music everywhere.

But she didn't hear the music. She heard only
one thing inside[6] her head. "Today you will die."

In the evening, they got onto the ship. They were sailing back to[7] the prince's home. It was filled with[8] food and music. On the deck, there were many colored[9] lights. The mermaid thought, "Like the first time I saw the prince."

That night, she danced for the prince and his bride. She danced very elegantly[10]. But her feet and her heart were in pain[11]. The prince did not know about her pain. After that night, she would not see the prince again.

1 **wear** [wɛr] (v.) 穿著 (wear-wore-worn)
2 **golden** [ˈɡoldn̩] (a.) 金色的
3 **behind** [bɪˈhaɪnd] (prep.) 在……後面
4 **bride** [braɪd] (n.) 新娘
5 **joyful** [ˈdʒɔɪfəl] (a.) 令人喜悅的
6 **inside** [ɪnˈsaɪd] (prep.) 在內的
7 **sail back to** 航行回到
8 **be filled with** 充滿著
9 **colored** [ˈkʌləd] (a.) 有顏色的
10 **elegantly** [ˈɛləɡəntlɪ] (adv.) 優雅地；高雅地
11 **in pain** 痛苦地

One Point Lesson

◊ Like **the first time** (that) I saw the prince.
就像我初次見到王子那時一樣。

that 後面接的是關係子句，用來修飾 that 前面的 the first time

the first time (that) | I saw the prince |
先行詞　　　　　　　關係子句

e.g. You have **the book** (that) I really wanted to buy.
你擁有的那本書就是我很想要買的那一本。

25

Everything on the ship became very quiet[1]. The mermaid walked quietly[2] along[3] the deck.

She looked out into the water. "This is my last[4] night," she thought. "In the morning, I will die."

Then, she saw something in the water. It was her sisters. They looked different. Their beautiful hair was gone[5].

"We all cut[6] our hair," they said to her. "We sold[7] it to the witch. We brought[8] you something to help you."

---

1 **quiet** [kwaɪət] (a.) 安靜的
2 **quietly** [ˋkwaɪətlɪ] (adv.) 安靜地
3 **along** [əˋlɔŋ] (prep.) 沿著
4 **last** [læst] (a.) 最後的
5 **be gone** 消失
6 **cut** [kʌt] (v.) 剪短
7 **sell** [sɛl] (v.) 賣
   (sell-sold-sold)

8 **bring** [brɪŋ] (v.) 帶來
   (bring-brought-brought)
9 **kill** [kɪl] (v.) 殺死
10 **then** [ðɛn] (adv.) 然後
11 **take** [tek] (v.) 拿；取
12 **sharp** [ʃɑrp] (a.) 鋒利的

"It is a knife. Kill[9] the prince. Then[10],
you will not die. You can become a mermaid
again. You can live with us again."

She took[11] the knife from them. It was
very, very sharp[12].

26

She walked toward the prince's room. She went to the prince and his bride. They were sleeping peacefully[1]. They were asleep[2] in each other's arms[3].

The little mermaid leaned down[4], and kissed his cheek.

She looked at the knife. Then, she looked at the prince. No, she couldn't kill the prince. She loved him.

1 **peacefully** ['pisfulɪ] (adv.)
平靜地；和平地

2 **asleep** [ə'slip] (a.) 睡著的

3 **in one's arm** 在某人臂彎中

4 **lean down** 屈身
(lean-leaned-leaned)

5 **throw** [θro] (v.) 拋；扔
(throw-threw-thrown)

6 **through** [θru] (prep.) 通過

7 **drop** [drɑp] (v.) 落下
(drop-dropped-dropped)

8 **fall** [fɔl] (v.) 落下

9 **rise** [raɪz] (v.) 上升

So, she threw[5] the knife through[6] the window. It dropped[7] into the sea. She watched it fall[8].

She looked into the sky. The sun was rising[9]. She quickly ran to the deck. She threw herself into the sea. She felt the cold water. "I am dying," she thought.

One Point Lesson

● She **watched** it **fall**. 她看著它落下。

「感官動詞（see, watch, hear, feel, notice 等）＋ 受詞 ＋ 動詞」，此句型中，受詞後面的動詞須接原形動詞或動名詞，不可用不定詞（to ＋ 動詞原形）。這時這個動詞當受詞補語用。

e.g I **heard** him **call** my name. 我聽到他叫我的名字。

27

Suddenly, the little mermaid felt[1] herself above the water. She felt her body. She was in the air[2]. She saw other beautiful beings[3].

"Where am I? Who are you? What is happening[4]?" she asked them.

"We are the daughters of the air," they told her. "We give life to people. We carry[5] the sweet smell of flowers and perfume[6]. You are now a daughter of the air."

1 **feel** [fil] (v.) 感覺；覺得
2 **air** [ɛr] (n.) 天空；空中
3 **being** [ˋbiɪŋ] (n.) 人；生物
4 **happen** [ˋhæpən] (v.) 發生
5 **carry** [ˋkærɪ] (v.) 傳送
6 **perfume** [ˋpɝfjum] (n.) 芳香
7 **hard** [hɑrd] (adv.) 努力地
8 **earn** [ɝn] (v.) 獲得
9 **soul** [sol] (n.) 靈魂
10 **by** [baɪ] (prep.) 藉由；因

"You were a mermaid," they continued. "You tried so hard[7] to earn[8] a soul[9].The daughters of the air can live for three hundred years. But by[10] doing good, we can earn a soul."

"I can earn a soul? This is wonderful." She looked into the sky and thought, "Thank you. Thank you."

Now, she looked toward the ship.
It was sailing calmly[1] on the ocean.
Then, she saw the prince and his bride.
They were looking for[2] her. Their faces
were white[3]. They looked into the sea.
They looked so sad.

The Little Mermaid

The little mermaid went to them. Of course[4], they could not see her. She moved her body around[5] them. They felt the cool air move around them. She kissed the prince and his bride.

Then, she flew away[6]. She joined[7] her sisters in the air. They went for[8] doing good together. Three hundred years from now, the little mermaid will get a soul.

1 **calmly** [ˈkɑmlɪ] (adv.) 平靜地
2 **look for** 尋找
3 **white** [hwaɪt] (a.) 蒼白的
4 **of course** 當然

5 **around** [əˈraʊnd] (prep.) 在附近
6 **fly away** 飛走
7 **join** [dʒɔɪn] (v.) 加入
8 **go for** 追求；試圖

A Complete the sentences with antonyms of the words underlined.

❶ The little mermaid's sisters swam _____ to the ship.
↳ *far*

❷ The little mermaid was _____ to be with the prince.
↳ *sad*

❸ At the wedding, the little mermaid walked _____ the bride.
↳ *before*

❹ The little mermaid could _____ if she killed the prince.
↳ *die*

B Fill in the blanks with the given words.

took	die	become

"It is a knife. Kill the prince. Then, you will not ❶_____. You can ❷_____ a mermaid again." said the sisters. She ❸_____ the knife from them. She walked toward the prince's room.

Appendixes

1 Basic Grammar

要增強英文閱讀理解能力，應練習找出英文的主結構。

要擁有良好的英語閱讀能力，首先要理解英文的段落結構。

「英文的閱讀理解從「分解文章」開始」

英文的文章是以「有意義的詞組」（指帶有意義的語句）所構成的。用（／）符號來區別各個意義語塊，請試著掌握其中的意義。

主詞	動詞
某樣東西（人、事、物）	如何做

He runs (very fast).　　It is raining.

他　跑　（非常快）　　　雨　正在下

主詞	動詞	補語（補充的話）
某樣東西（人、事、物）	如何做	怎麼樣

This is a cat.　　The cat is very big.

這　是 一隻貓。　　那隻貓　是 非常 大

主詞	動詞	受詞
某樣東西（人、事、物）	如何做	什麼

人、事物兩者皆是受詞

I like you.　　You gave me some flowers.

我 喜歡 你。　　你　給　我　一些花

主詞	動詞	受詞	補語
某樣東西 （人、事、物）	如何做	什麼	怎麼樣／什麼

You make me happy .

你　　使（讓）我　　快樂

I saw him running .

我 看到　他　　跑

其他修飾語或副詞等，都可以視為為了完成句子而額外、特別附加的，閱讀起來便可更加輕鬆；先具備這些基本概念，再閱讀部分精選篇章，最後做了解文章整體架構的練習。

Each sea-princess was very special .

每一位海裡的公主　　是　非常　特別的

But the youngest was the prettiest .

但是 年紀最小的　　是　　最漂亮的

Her skin was so white and clear , and

她的皮膚　是 如此　白　和 潔淨的 而且

her long hair flew smoothly in the sea.

　她的長髮　飛揚 流暢地　在海裡

She seemed like other girls on land.

她　　看起來　像其他女孩　在陸地上

But she had a tail like a fish.

但　她　有　尾巴　像魚

89

Every day the little mermaid liked to stay in her garden

　　每天　　　　小美人魚　喜歡　　待在　她的花園裡

and grew red flowers.

並　　種　紅色的 花朵

She never went out of the sea.

她　　從未　　去　海以外

One day, a beautiful statue fell to the bottom of the ocean.

一天　　　　美麗的雕像　　　落下　　　到海底

It looked like a beautiful boy.

它　看起來　像一個好看的男生

She asked her grandmother , " What is it ?"

她　　問　　她祖母　　　　什麼 是 它

" It is a statue from a ship on the ocean.

它 是　雕像　　從船上來　　在海上

It is like the people above us," replied her grandmother .

它 是　像人類　　　在我們上方　回答　　她祖母

At last, It was her oldest sister's birthday .

最後　這 是　　她大姊的生日

" It was wonderful ," she said .

這　是　美妙的　　她　說

" I saw so many things .

我 看到 如此多事物

I lay on a beach in the moonlight.

我 躺 海灘上 月光下

I saw a town and some people . It was so exciting ."

我 看到 一座城和一些人 那 是 如此 令人興奮的

The little mermaid listened carefully.

小美人魚 聽 仔細地

One year passed by quickly.

一年 過去 很快地

Now, It was the second sister's turn . She swam up a river.

現在 這 是 輪到二姊 她 游 上 一條河

She saw palaces, and green hills .

她 看到 皇宮和綠色的山丘

She saw people laughing and children playing .

她 看到 人類 笑 和兒童 遊玩

" It was interesting ," she said .

它 是 有趣的 她 說

" I want to go again tomorrow."

我 想要 去 再一次 明天

Guide to Listening Comprehension

 When listening to the story, use some of the techniques shown below. If you take time to study some phonetic characteristics of English, listening will be easier.

Get in the flow of English.

English creates a rhythm formed by combinations of strong and weak stress intonations. Each word has its particular stress that combines with other words to form the overall pattern of stress or rhythm in a particular sentence.

When you are speaking and listening to English, it is essential to get in the flow of the rhythm of English. It takes a lot of practice to get used to such a rhythm. So, you need to start by identifying the stressed syllable in a word.

Listen for the strongly stressed words and phrases.

In English, key words and phrases that are essential to the meaning of a sentence are stressed louder. Therefore, pay attention to the words stressed with a higher pitch. When listening to an English recording for the first time, what matters most is to listen for a general understanding of what you hear. Do not try to hear every single word. Most of the unstressed words are articles or auxiliary verbs, which don't play an important role in the general context. At this level, you can ignore them.

Pay attention to liaisons.

In reading English, words are written with a space between them. There isn't such an obvious guide when it comes to listening to English. In oral English, there are many cases when the sounds of words are linked with adjacent words.

For instance, let's think about the phrase "take off," which can be used in "take off your clothes." "Take off your clothes" doesn't sound like [teɪk ɔf] with each of the words completely and clearly separated from the others. Instead, it sounds as if almost all the words in context are slurred together, [ˈtekɔf], for a more natural sound.

Shadow the voice of the native speaker.

Finally, you need to mimic the voice of the native speaker. Once you are sure you know how to pronounce all the words in a sentence, try to repeat them like an echo. Listen to the book again, but this time you should try a fun exercise while listening to the English.

This exercise is called "shadowing." The word "shadow" means a dark shade that is formed on a surface. When used as a verb, the word refers to the action of following someone or something like a shadow. In this exercise, pretend you are a parrot and try to shadow the voice of the native speaker.

Try to mimic the reader's voice by speaking at the same speed, with the same strong and weak stresses on words, and pausing or stopping at the same points.

Experts have already proven this technique to be effective. If you practice this shadowing exercise, your English speaking and listening skills will improve by leaps and bounds. While shadowing the native speaker, don't forget to pay attention to the meaning of each phrase and sentence.

Step 1 Listen to what you want to shadow many times. Start out by just trying to shadow a few words or a sentence.

 Step 2 Mimic the CD out loud. You can shadow everything the speaker says as if you are singing a round, or you also can speak simultaneously with the recorded voice of the native speaker.

 Step 3 As you practice more, try to shadow more. For instance, shadow a whole sentence or paragraph instead of just a few words.

Listening Guide

以下為本書各章節的前半部。一開始若能聽清楚發音，之後就沒有聽力的負擔。首先，請聽過摘錄的章節，之後再反覆聆聽括弧內單字的發音，並仔細閱讀各種發音的說明。以下都是以英語的典型發音為基礎，所做的簡易說明，即使這裡未提到的發音，也可以反覆聆聽，如此一來，聽力必能更上層樓。

🎧 29 Chapter One page 14

> The (　①　) was a wonderful place. The (　②　) was a very beautiful blue. At the (　③　) of the ocean was an even more (　④　) world. There were so many wonderful sea creatures.

① **ocean**：重音在第一音節，需注意 c 發 [ʃ] 音。

② **water**：位於兩個母音中間的 t，會發 [d] 的音，這是頗具代表的美式發音。

③ **bottom**：這個字的 t 與前一個單字 (water) 相同，都位在兩個母音的中間，因此口語發音通常也會將 t 發作 [d] 音。

④ **amazing**：重音在第二音節，相對來說在重音節周圍的發音聽起來會較微弱，特別是當重音在第二音節，而第一音節是母音時，第一音節容易被忽略而聽不出正確的發音。

> The little mermaid finally (　❶　) fifteen. "I am (　❷　)! I am fifteen!" she shouted excitedly. Her (　❸　) put some white flowers in her hair.

❶ **became**：重音在第二音節，所以字首 be- 的發音聽起來微弱，不注意聽的話甚至會把單字誤聽為 came。

❷ **fifteen**：fifteen (15) 和 fifty (50) 常讓英語學習者分不清楚發音，其實 fifteen 的重音在後，[i] 的發音會比較清楚，而 fifty 的重音在前，字尾的 [i] 音通常不太清楚，可以此做判斷。

❸ **grandmother**：這個單字較長，有三個音節，重音在第一音節。其中 grand- 的 d，發音微弱，在口語中通常會聽不清楚甚至省略，而 d 和 mother 之間會有極短暫的停頓。

> The little mermaid (　❶　) (　　) look for the witch. She swam to a very dark place. She thought, "This is a very (　❷　) place. But I must go." She continued to swim. She saw many whirlpools. She (　❸　) (　　) be careful. A whirlpool could suck her into its middle.

❶ **want to**：want 的 t 和 to 的 t 連在一起發音，此時 to 的音聽起來就像 [tə]，在英語中若相同的兩個音連在一起時只需發音一次。

❷ **scary**：p、k、t 等字母若接在 s 後，則這些子音會發不送氣音（即有聲子音，如 [b]、[d] 等），聽起來會類似 [b]、[g]、[d] 的音。

❸ **had to**：除了在特別強調的時候以外，to 在會話中通常會變成 [t] 的音，而 had 的 d 發音也很輕，整句聽起來就像 [hæt]。

In the morning, the little mermaid (❶) ( ),
and (❷) ( ) her body. Her tail was gone.
Now, she had two legs (❸) two feet. Then she
saw a shadow. She looked up. The prince was standing
over her and staring at her face. The prince asked
(❹), "Who are you? Where are you from?"

❶ **woke up**：以 k 結尾的單字後面接 up 時，形成連音，變成 wo kup。

❷ **looked at**：looked 的 -ed 接在 k 後面，發無聲子音，發音為 [lʊkt]。

❸ **and**：連接詞 and 通常發音微弱，只聽得到 n 的音，但連接句子；位
於句首或用於強調時，就需要清楚地發音。

❹ **her**：通常以 h 開頭的代名詞（his、him、her 等），依前後文迅速
發弱音時，[h] 因會迅速略過聽不清楚。

A (**❶**) ( ) (**❷**), she heard some news. The prince planned to marry a king's daughter. "I must go to meet the king's daughter," he said to the mermaid. She felt very (**❸**) ( ) this. My parents (**❹**) ( ) to go. I do not want to marry her," he said. This made her very happy.

❶ short time：相同的音（[t]）連在一起，因此只發音一次。

❷ later：t 的前後字母皆為母音，故此時 t 發 [d] 的音。

❸ sad about：about 的重音在 -bout 上，a- 的音往往發得很輕。

❹ want me：兩個單字連起來發音，此時 want 的 [t] 音非常迅速帶過，聽起來像是沒有發音。

4

Listening Comprehension

🎧 34 **A** Listen to the CD and circle the correct word.

1 The prince was (thinking / sinking) deep into the ocean.

2 Everything on the (sheep / ship) became very quiet.

3 She joined her sisters in (the air / there).

4 They were (asleep / sleep) in each other's arms.

5 The branches (floor / float) around the statue's (face / pace).

6 With our good (did / deeds), we can earn a soul.

🎧 35 **B** Write down the sentences and circle either True or False.

1 T F _____

2 T F _____

3 T F _____

4 T F _____

5 T F _____

C Listen to the CD, write down the question and choose the correct answer.

❶ _____?

    (a) She became a person.

    (b) She became a sea witch.

    (c) She died last year.

    (d) She died a long time ago.

❷ _____?

    (a) The prince's mother.

    (b) The priest of the temple.

    (c) The young girl from the village.

    (d) A young girl from the temple.

❸ _____?

    (a) Dead fish bones.

    (b) Dead mermaid bones.

    (c) Seashells.

    (d) Dead sailor's bones.

❹ _____?

    (a) He loved her like a sister.

    (b) He loved her like a wife.

    (c) He loved her like his mother.

    (d) He loved her like his girlfriend.

Translation

作者簡介

P. 4 1805 年 4 月 2 日，漢斯·克里斯汀·安徒生出生於歐登塞菲英島上的一個小漁村，父親是個窮鞋匠。不過父親喜愛文學、思想先進，他自己喜歡閱讀，也鼓勵兒子安徒生培養自己的文藝興趣。

安徒生在大學時代開始寫作，他的第一本小説《即興詩人》（*The Improvisatore*），以自己 1833 年在義大利的旅遊經歷為題材，這本小説佳評如潮，享有的聲譽甚至更勝於他的第一部童話故事《講給孩子們聽的故事》（*Tales Told for Children*）。

後來，安徒生成為深受喜愛的兒童文學作家。1875 年，安徒生辭世，出版的故事共計一百三十餘則。

安徒生的許多著作被視為是最優異的兒童文學作品，例如《美人魚》（*The Little Mermaid*）、《醜小鴨》（*The Ugly Duckling*）、《國王的新衣》（*The Emperor' New Clothes*）。儘管遭遇諸多困難，安徒生克服了各種挑戰，成為成功的作家。安徒生在作品中熱衷於透過抒情詩意的筆觸，來展現美麗虛幻的幻想世界和人道主義。

安徒生過著獨居生活，並於 1875 年孤獨離世。在他的出殯日，丹麥舉國上下都穿著喪服，國王和皇后並親赴葬禮。安徒生也是一位活躍的詩人，而他美麗的童話故事仍受到世界各地人們的喜愛。

故事簡介

P. 5 安徒生終生愛著一位女子，並根據這場無疾而終的愛戀寫成《小美人魚》（*The Little Mermaid*）。

15 歲生日那天，小美人魚第一次被允許游出海面。在那兒，她瞧見在船上慶祝生日的王子，並墜入愛情。正當她看得出神，一陣突如的風暴掃過海面，摧毀了遊船。然而，小美人魚將失去意識的王子從船難救起。

為了接近王子，小美人魚與海妖交易。她以自己的聲音交換，變成人類，前往王子的宮殿。但是王子並不知道失去聲音的小美人魚才是他的救命恩人，迎娶了鄰國的公主。絕望下，小美人魚跳入海裡，並幻化成空中的仙子。

安徒生許多動人的童話中，以《小美人魚》最廣為傳閱，並觸動世上大人與小孩的心。

[第一章] 海底世界

P. 14–15　海洋真是個美妙的地方！
海水蔚藍美麗，而海底，更讓人感到
驚異不已。

那兒有許多奇異的海中生物，甚至
還有一位海裡的國王，他居住在海底的城
堡中，他的城堡比陸地上的任何城堡都更美輪美奐。

國王與六位公主生活在一起，皇后在多年前去世，由公主的祖母這位充滿智慧的女性，照顧她們的生活。

美麗的公主們成天聚在一起游泳，也會和海中的魚兒一同玩樂，海裡的魚兒就像是空中的飛鳥。

P. 16–17　每一位公主都有獨特之處，年紀最輕的公主是其中最美麗的。她的肌膚柔白光滑，秀髮隨水流飛揚，外表看起來與生長在陸地上的女孩無異，只是身上長著和魚一樣的尾鰭。

這位小美人魚喜歡每天待在花園裡，種植紅色的花朵，她從未離開過大海。

有一天，一座雕像沉入海底深處，雕像刻的是一名俊美男子。

小美人魚問祖母：「那是什麼？」

「那是一座從船上掉落水中的雕像，刻的似乎是住在陸地上的人類。」祖母這麼說著。

小美人魚很喜歡這座雕像，還在它周圍種了一些美麗的樹木，枝葉漂浮在雕像的臉旁。在這片深不可測的海底，他總是面帶微笑。

P. 18–19 小美人魚很愛聽陸地上的故事，她總是對祖母說：「跟我說說陸地上發生的故事吧。」祖母訴說著美麗的船隻、城鎮和陸地上人類的事情。

「真的嗎？花會散發香味？樹上的魚會唱歌？」小美人魚問著，不知道鳥兒的存在。

「我想要看看人類、看那裡的魚，和那裡的花。」她說道。

「等妳滿十五歲就可以去了。」祖母對她說。

「十五歲！」小美人魚想著，「現在我才九歲，還得等好久啊！」

小美人魚游向大姊身邊。「大姊！」她說「妳明年就滿十五歲了，要把陸地上的一切都告訴我喔。」

P. 20–21 終於，大姊十五歲生日到了。

「太美妙了！」大姊說，「我看到好多東西。我在月光下躺在海邊，看到一座城和一些人類，好有趣啊！」小美人魚專注地聽著。

一年很快地過去，現在又到了二姊的生日，她游到小河上，看到了一座宮殿和幾座綠色的小山丘，還見到大人們開懷大笑、小孩子們玩樂嬉戲。

「實在是有趣極了！」二姊說，「我明天還想再去一次。」又一次，小美人魚覺得羨慕不已。

P. 22–23 每一年都會有一個姊姊對其他姊妹訴說陸地上的世界，她們愛看新的事物，只不過一下子就膩了。

但是小美人魚想要看到一切，她總是對姊姊們說，「再跟我說說別的事。」

「我們已經把一切都告訴妳，無可奉告了，陸地上沒什麼好玩的了。」她們說。

每一晚，小美人魚抬頭望，想著，「什麼時候才輪到我呢？」

「我想要快點十五歲，姊姊都不在乎陸地上的世界，但是我會永遠愛那片陸地。」她對自己說。

[第二章] 陸地上的世界

P. 28–29 終於，小美人魚十五歲了。「我十五歲了！我十五歲了！」她興奮地叫喊。祖母在她的頭髮別上幾朵白色的小花。

接著，她游向海面，現在正是夕陽西下時分，空中布滿橘紅色的雲朵。「好美啊！」她想。

看見船隻在海面上航行，她游向船邊，聽見了音樂聲與笑語。

船上也有一個年輕人，他是王子，大家正在為他舉辦一場生日宴會，他們看起來全都非常開心。

小美人魚盯著王子看了好幾個小時。

P. 30–31 突然間，一陣暴風雨來襲，天空變得陰暗，狂風大作，海面上波濤洶湧。

小美人魚並不害怕，在暴風雨中游泳對她來說很有趣，但對船隻就完全不是那麼回事。一陣強風呼呼地吹過，吹斷了船桅，沒過多久，船身便被大海覆蓋淹沒了。

小美人魚看到許多人在湍急的海浪中拼命游著。

「人類的泳技不太好，王子在哪裡？我得去救他。」她想。

過了一會兒，她找到了王子，王子正緩緩地沈入深海中。她帶著王子浮上海面，一整晚都在看著他英俊的臉龐。

P. 32–33 到了清晨，暴風雨已經平息。在陽光的照耀下，王子看起來更加英俊，但他的雙眼依然緊閉著。

「請你千萬別死！一定要活下來。」她說道。

離海邊不遠處，有一間小屋。她將王子帶到小屋旁邊，讓他躺在那兒的海灘上。

這時突然響起陣陣鐘聲，一群年輕女孩從小屋走了出來。

其中一個女孩看到了倒在海邊的王子，便走向他。接著，女孩跑著去求救，沒過多久，就有許多人來將王子帶走了。

一時之間，小美人魚覺得十分落寞。

P. 34–35 小美人魚回到家後，她的姊姊全都喊著，「妳看到什麼了？看到什麼了？」

但是小美人魚不發一語，她傷心地說不出話來。

終於有一天，她把事情告訴姊姊們，其中一位姊姊帶她到王子的宮殿前，她又找到她的王子了！

「我隨時都可以到這兒來！」現在她這麼想著。

有許許多多個夜晚，她都待在這兒。

過了一段時間，她對人類有太多好奇和疑問，她決定要問問祖母。

「奶奶，人類可以長生不死嗎？」她問。

「不行，但是他們可以活很久，而且他們的靈魂是永恆不朽的。至於我們人魚，能夠活三百歲，三百年後就會化成海裡的泡沫。」

P. 36–37 「我想要有靈魂，我想要像人類一樣生活。」小美人魚說，「我永遠都不能有靈魂嗎？我要怎麼做才能擁有靈魂呢？」她問祖母。

祖母說，「只有一個方法，就是必須要有人類愛上妳，和妳結婚。但這是不可能的，妳有一條美麗的魚尾，但人類覺得它很醜，沒有人會想娶一條人魚的。別再幻想陸地上的生活了，妳終究只會讓自己傷心的。」

她看著自己的魚尾想，「我討厭它，我想要一雙腿，我想要嫁給王子。」

「快樂一點吧，」最後祖母説道，「開開心心地活這三百年。今晚有一場盛大的宴會，到時妳的心情就會變好了。」

P.38-39 深海城堡裡的宴會奇幻美好，牆上有各式各樣的貝殼裝飾。

美人魚和男人魚在宴會廳中跳舞歡唱，他們都有美好的嗓音，尤以小美人魚的聲音最美，大家都愛聽她唱歌。在那一段短暫的時間裡，小美人魚覺得很開心。

但是，接著她想到王子，又難過了起來。她傷心地離開舞會，來到屬於她自己的地方——她的花園。在那裡，她可以靜靜地哭泣。她想著，「我愛他，願意為他做任何事，我要去找海巫，她可以幫我。」

[第三章] 海巫

P.44-45 小美人魚跑去找海巫，她游向海中最陰沈黑暗的地區。她想著：「這個地方好可怕，但是我一定要去。」她繼續游著，沿途看到許多漩渦，她得小心一點，不然可能會被捲入漩渦裡。

游了一段時間，她看到了海巫的房子，那是用許多死去水手的骨頭建造的，小公主很害怕，差一點就要離開。但接著她又想，「為了王子！為了我的靈魂！我不能害怕。」她游向海巫的家，甚至看到一名已死的年輕人魚躺在那兒。

小美人魚震驚不已，她又想離開了。

但海巫走出門口，説道：「別走！我知道妳為何而來。」

P. 46-47　小美人魚跟著海巫進入人骨建造的屋子。

　　「妳這個笨女孩，妳的家人會很傷心的。不過我會為妳實現願望，」海巫說。

　　「我會給妳一瓶飲料，妳把它帶在身邊，明天清晨日出前妳要游到陸地，坐在海灘上喝下魔藥。到時妳的尾巴就會消失，長出雙腿，但是妳會很痛，就好像有刀在割妳的雙腳一樣。不過妳可以走得很好，也能跳出美麗的舞步。妳能忍受得了這種痛苦嗎？」

P. 48-49　小美人魚對海巫說：「我能夠忍受下來的！」

　　海巫認真看著她，問道：「妳確定？從此妳再也無法變回人魚，再也無法與姊姊們一起游泳，再也無法見到父親和祖母了，而且妳一定要王子結婚才能擁有靈魂，如果他娶了別人，妳就會死去。妳真的確定要這樣做嗎？」

　　小美人魚說：「對，我確定。」她很害怕地答道。

　　「那麼，妳要給我報酬，我要妳的聲音。」海巫說，「反正妳不需要它了，王子會愛上妳的美貌的。」

　　「我的聲音？那我要怎麼說話呢？」小美人魚問。

　　「我就要這個報酬，」海巫突然吼道，「妳很美，你的雙眼很會替你發聲的。」

　　「那就這樣做吧。」小美人魚說。

P. 50-51　海巫開始製作魔藥，她把一些恐怖的東西全都加進藥裡。她先是加了魚胃，又加進螃蟹的眼睛，接著還加了烏賊腦。魔藥冒著煙，味道難聞。

　　「這就是要給妳的魔藥了，」海巫說，「現在妳得把舌頭交給我。」

　　小美人魚把舌頭伸出來，海巫將它割下，過程極痛苦。她想要說話，但卻一個字也說不出來。

海巫又對她説，「明天清晨，日出之前，照我説的話做，妳就會有一雙美麗的腿了。」

小美人魚想要説「我會的」，但卻發不出聲音。她只能點點頭，接著便離開了海巫的家。

P. 52–53 她很快回到家，大家都已經睡了。她想要去和姊姊們説説話，卻一個字也説不出來。

她現在很難過，只想哭。但是她沒有哭，反而來到花園。她從姊姊的花園裡摘了一些花，想要當作對姊姊和家園的回憶留念。接著，她便離開了。

小美人魚在水中游著，天就快要亮了，現在她能清楚看見一切事物。

她朝王子的宮殿游著，越來越接近。抵達海灘後，她便靠在那兒。接著，她喝下了魔藥。剎那間，她全身感到極度不舒服，就好像有一把刀在她體內。她倒在沙灘上。

[第四章] 新世界

P. 56–57 到了早晨，小美人魚甦醒，看了看自己的身體。她的尾巴消失了。現在，她有了雙腿和雙足。

接著她見到一道陰影，抬起頭。

王子就站在她的上方，正盯著她的臉瞧。

王子問她：「妳是誰？妳從哪裡來的？」

但是她無法回答，只能深深地望著他的雙眼，那一瞬間，王子對她油然生起一股強烈的情感。

王子説道：「先進來屋裡，妳一定很冷吧。」

她站起身，雙腿與雙足卻感受到一股劇烈的痛苦，但她不去想它。

王子帶著她來到皇宮，還給她一件漂亮的衣服穿，於是她成了宮中最美麗的女孩。

P. 58-59 幾天後，宮裡有一場歌唱比賽，許多美麗的女子前來獻唱，她們的歌聲都極為優美，但這對小美人魚來說卻是十分難熬，她想：「我也想為王子獻唱，我的嗓音比她們更加優美。」

沒過多久，宮裡又舉辦了一場舞會，這下小公主總算可以為王子獻舞了。她的舞姿是那麼的優雅動人，她用雙手傳達出內心的情感，雙眸中表現出的感情更加深刻。

在場所有人皆鼓掌喊著：「太美了！太棒了！」

王子的目光也無法從她身上移開。

P. 60-61 舞會結束後，她時時刻刻都與王子在一起。她會與他共乘一匹馬，他們一起騎乘穿越清新的森林、踏過平靜的海水。他們形影不離，但是她總是感到疼痛，她的雙腳不時地流血，她總是強忍著。

有時候，她會趁著夜晚來到海邊，把雙腳放進海水中，這會讓她覺得舒服多了。

在這樣的時刻，她會想起自己的親人，她想：「我希望他們過得快樂，希望他們都很健康，也希望他們都能諒解我。」

P. 62-63 一天夜裡，小美人魚來到海邊，把雙腳放進冰涼的海水裡。

突然間，她看到了姊姊們。

「姊姊！」她大聲呼喊，但她一點聲音也發不出來，於是她揮舞著雙手，希望她們會注意到她。終於她們轉過頭看到她了。

「妳沒有死！」姊姊說著，「我們到處在找妳，還為妳哭得那麼傷心。能見到妳我們實在太高興了。」

「我也很高興能見到妳們。」小美人魚想說。

之後的每一晚，她們都會來到這兒相見。

P. 64-65 小美人魚愛上了王子，王子也愛小美人魚，但卻是兩種不同的愛。

他把她當作妹妹一般疼愛，完全沒想過要娶她為妻，這讓她難過不已。

王子曾告訴她一個故事：「我曾在乘船出海時遇到暴風雨，船翻覆了，被淹沒海裡，我也被海浪沖到海邊，但一位年輕女孩在海邊發現我，救了我一命。

我只喜愛她一個人。妳長得很像她，說不定是她讓妳來到我身邊的。」

小美人魚非常傷心，「是我救了你，但是你卻不知道。」她想。

[第五章] 駭人的消息

P. 70-71 過了不久，她聽到一些消息，說王子將要娶另一位國王的女兒。

「我必須去與這位公主見面。」王子對小美人魚說，她聽了非常難過。

「我父母希望我去，可是我一點也不想娶她。」他說。這又讓小美人魚欣喜不已。

「和我一起去好嗎？我希望妳能和我一起坐船航行。」王子說道。

夜裡，小美人魚坐在甲板上，望著大海深處。

突然間，她的姊姊們出現了。她們本來要游向船邊，但一見到甲板上的王子，就又游回深海中了。

小美人魚感到非常失望。不過她還是很開心，因為她每天都能看見王子。

P. 72-73 大船來到一座美麗的城鎮，公主便住在這裡，許多人湧至船邊迎接王子的到來。城裡一整天都在舉行慶典，但公主一整天都沒有出現。

但到了晚上，她出現了，王子認出公主的容貌。「是妳！」他高喊著，「就是妳！是妳救了我的命！」

王子看著小美人魚，說道：「喔！我實在太開心了！這一切是那麼完美，我深愛這個女人，而妳又陪在我身邊，我的生活毫無遺憾了。」小美人魚對他微笑，但她的心已經裂成兩半。他的婚禮只意味著一件事：她的死亡。

P. 74–75 為了參加王子與公主的婚禮，小美人魚穿了一件金色的禮服。在教堂中，她走在新娘的後面，歡樂的樂聲四處響起。

但是她聽不見音樂，腦中只有一個念頭：「今天妳將面臨死亡。」

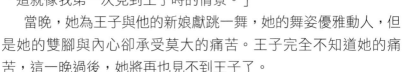

傍晚時分，他們上了船，準備啟程回到王子的家鄉。船上到處都是美食與樂聲，甲板上點了各色的燈光。小美人魚心想，「這就像我第一次見到王子時的情景。」

當晚，她為王子與他的新娘獻跳一舞，她的舞姿優雅動人，但是她的雙腳與內心卻承受莫大的痛苦。王子完全不知道她的痛苦，這一晚過後，她將再也見不到王子了。

P. 76–77 此刻，船上一片沈靜。小美人魚默默走在甲板上。

她往外望著大海。「這是我的最後一晚，」她想著，「到了明天一早，我就會死。」

接著，她見到水中出現的身影。那是她的姊姊們，她們看起來和以前不同，原本一頭美麗的長髮全都不見了。

「我們剪下自己的頭髮，」她們對她說，「賣給海巫，帶了一樣東西來幫妳。」

「這是一把刀，用它殺了王子，妳就可以免於一死了。妳可以變回人魚，再跟我們一起生活。」

小美人魚從姊姊手中接過那把刀，那是一把非常非常鋒利的刀。

P. 78–79 她走到王子房裡，走向王子與他的新娘，他們平靜地睡著，沈睡在彼此的懷中。

小美人魚彎下身，親吻王子的臉頰。

她看著那把刀，再看看王子。不，她沒辦法殺害王子，她愛他。

於是，她把刀扔出窗外，看著刀子落入海中。她抬頭望向天空，太陽已漸漸升起，她迅速跑向甲板，接著便投身海中。她感覺到海水的冰冷，「我就要死了。」她想。

P. 80–81 突然間，小美人魚感覺自己離開了水面。她可以感覺到自己的身體，現在她身在空中，還看見其他美麗的人物。

「這兒是那裡？你們又是誰？到底發生了什麼事？」她問。

「我們是天空的女兒，」他們告訴她，「我們為人們帶來生命，為花朵傳遞甜美的芳香。現在妳也成為天空的女兒了。」

「妳原本是一條人魚，卻那麼努力地想要得到靈魂。」她們繼續說道，「天空的女兒能夠活三百年，但只要不斷行善，我們也能得到靈魂。」

「我可以得到靈魂？太棒了。」她看著天空想，「謝謝你！謝謝你！」

P. 82–83 現在她望著那艘船，它平靜地航駛在海洋中，接著她看到了王子與他的新娘，他們正在找她。他們臉色蒼白，望著大海，神情是那麼哀傷。

小美人魚來到他們身邊，當然他們看不到她。她在他們身邊舞動著身體，他們感受到涼爽的空氣在身旁流過。她親吻了王子與他的新娘。

接著她便飛走了。她飛回空中加入姊妹的行列，她們要一起行善，從現在起到往後三百年間，小美人魚將努力獲得靈魂。

List of words 用字表

a
about
above
afraid
after
again
age
ago
air
aisle
all
almost
along
also
always
am
amaze
an
and
angry
another
answer
any
anymore
anything
appear
are
arm
around
as
ask
asleep
at
attention
away

awful
baby
back
ballroom
band
be
beach
bear
beautiful
beautifully
beauty
become
before
begin
behind
bell
beside
best
big
bird
birthday
blank
bleed
blue
board
boat
body
boil
bone
book
bore
bother
bottle
bottom
bouquet

boy
brain
branch
break
bride
bridegroom
bridesmaid
bring
broken
build
but
buy
by
call
calm
calmly
can
candle
cannot
care
careful
carefully
carry
castle
celebrate
ceremony
chapter
cheek
cheerful
child
choose
chronological
church
clap
clear

clearly
close
clothe
cloud
cold
color
come
complete
comprehension
contest
continue
continuous
cool
coral
correct
course
crab
creature
cross
crosswords
crown
cry
cut
dance
dancer
dark
daughter
day
dead
decide
deck
decorate
deep
deeply
die

even	find	guest	in
different	finally	hair	inside
difficult	finish	hand	instead
disappear	fire	handsome	interest
disappoint	first	happen	into
do	fish	happily	it
door	five	happy	its
down	flow	hard	join
dream	flower	hate	just
dress	fly	have	kill
drink	foam	he	kind
drop	follow	if	king
each	food	head	kiss
earn	foot	hear	knife
eat	for	help	look
elegant	forest	her	land
elegantly	forever	here	last
English	four	herself	late
envious	French	hide	laugh
every	fresh	hill	laughter
everyone	friend	him	lay
everything	from	his	lean
everywhere	full	joyful	least
excite	fun	hold	leave
excitedly	garden	home	leg
express	get	hope	lie
eye	girl	horse	life
face	give	hot	mermaid
fall	glad	hour	light
family	glass	house	like
float	go	know	listen
fan	golden	how	live
fantastic	graceful	human	long
far	grade	hundred	lot
father	heart	hurriedly	love
feel	grandmother	hurry	make
festival	great	I	man
few	green	ignore	many
fifteen	girl	laughter	marriage
fill	grow	impossible	marry

mast	off	sailor	sell
maybe	often	princess	send
me	oh	purpose	sentence
mean	old	purposely	set
medicine	on	put	shadow
meet	once	question	sharp
memory	one	quickly	special
merman	only	quiet	she
middle	onto	quietly	shell
minute	or	quiz	stand
moment	order	reach	shock
moonlight	other	see	short
morning	our	read	shout
mother	over	really	sick
oneself	own	rearrange	sing
move	pain	reception	sink
music	run	red	sister
orange	painful	rescue	strange
must	palace	rest	sit
my	parent	return	six
out	party	rewrite	skeleton
name	pass	ride	skin
near	past	ship	sky
need	pay	ring	sleep
never	peace	rise	small
new	peacefully	river	smell
news	people	rock	smile
next	pepper	rough	smoothly
night	perfume	sad	snap
nine	person	sadly	so
no	place	sail	some
nod	plan	sand	something
noise	plant	save	tell
not	play	say	sometimes
nothing	room	scare	sorrow
notice	please	scary	sorry
perfect	pot	sea	soul
now	pretty	search	sound
ocean	price	second	speak
of	prince	seem	spend

squid	their	way
star	them	we
stare	then	wear
thing	there	wed
starfish	they	weed
start	think	week
statue	this	welcome
stay	three	what
stick	through	when
still	throw	where
stomach	time	whirlpool
stop	to	white
storm	today	who
story	together	why
strong	tomorrow	wife
study	tongue	will
stupid	too	wind
such	top	window
suck	toward	wise
suddenly	town	wish
sun	tree	witch
sunlight	try	with
sunrise	two	woman
sunset	ugly	wonderful
sure	underline	word
turn	understand	world
sweet	up	year
swim	us	yes
under	use	yet
tail	very	you
take	voice	young
teenager	write	your
temple	wait	
tennis	wake	
tense	walk	
terrible	wall	
than	want	
thank	watch	
that	water	
the	wave	

Answers

P. 24

(A)
❶ mermaid **❷** squid **❸** sea creatures
❹ fish **❺** crab

(B) **❶** T **❷** F **❸** F **❹** T

P. 25

(C) **❶** was **❷** took **❸** swam **❹** fell

(D)
❶ the prettiest **❷** like other girls **❸** feet
❹ like a fish **❺** to play

P. 40

(A) mast, crown, cloud, building, castle,

(B) **❶** decorated **❷** beautifully **❸** soul

P. 41

(C) **❶** c **❷** b

(D) **❶** → **❸** → **❷** → **❹**

P. 54

(A)
❶ tongue **❷** voice **❸** sound
❹ pain **❺** painful

(B) **❶** T **❷** F **❸** F

P. 55

(C)
❶ so many **❷** so much **❸** So many
❹ so much

(D) **❶** witch **❷** scary **❸** suck

P. 66   (A)   **1** looking   **2** wearing   **3** dancing
               4 riding

        (B)   **1** F   **2** T   **3** T

P. 67   (C)   **1** The prince was standing over her.
               2 He was staring at her face.
               3 She was wearing very beautiful clothes.

        (D)   **3** → **4** → **5** → **2** → **1**

P. 84   (A)   **1** close   **2** happy   **3** behind   **4** live

        (B)   **1** die   **2** become   **3** took

P. 100   (A)   **1** sinking   **2** ship   **3** the air
               4 asleep   **5** float / face   **6** deeds

        (B)   **1** The Sea King lives with six sea-princesses and his mother. (T)
               2 The witch cut off the sisters' tongue. (F)
               3 The mermaid danced gracefully for the prince. (T)
               4 The prince wanted to marry the little mermaid. (F)
               5 The little mermaid killed the prince and became a mermaid again. (F)

P. 101   (C)   **1** What happened to the little mermaid's mother? (d)
               2 Who found the prince on the beach? (d)
               3 What was the witch's house made from? (d)
               4 How did the prince feel about the little mermaid? (a)

Adaptors of *The Little Mermaid*

Louise Benette

Macquarie University (MA, TESOL)
Sookmyung Women's University, English Instructor

David Hwang

Michigan State University (MA, TESOL)
Ewha Womans University, English Chief Instructor, CEO
at EDITUS

小美人魚【二版】
The Little Mermaid

作者 _ 漢斯·克里斯汀·安徒生
　　　（Hans Christian Andersen）
改寫 _ Louise Benette, David Hwang
插圖 _ Ekaterina Andreeva
翻譯 / 編輯 _ 羅竹君
作者 / 故事簡介翻譯 _ 王采翎
校對 _ 王采翎 / 洪巧玲
封面設計 _ 林書玉
排版 _ 葳豐 / 林書玉
播音員 _ Kate Ferguson / Michael Yancey
製程管理 _ 洪巧玲
發行人 _ 周均亮
出版者 _ 寂天文化事業股份有限公司
電話 _ +886-2-2365-9739
傳真 _ +886-2-2365-9835
網址 _ www.icosmos.com.tw
讀者服務 _ onlineservice@icosmos.com.tw
出版日期 _ 2019年7月 二版一刷（250201）
郵撥帳號 _ 1998620-0 寂天文化事業股份有限公司

國家圖書館出版品預行編目資料

小美人魚 / Hans Christian Andersen 原著 ; Louise
Benette, David Hwang 改編 . -- 二版 . -- [臺北市]
: 寂天文化, 2019.07
面；公分 . -- (Grade 1 經典文學讀本)
譯自：The little mermaid
ISBN 978-986-318-817-9 (25K 平裝附光碟片)
1. 英語 2. 讀本
805.18   108010572